Puppy
To The Rescue

Written by Kay Barnes
Illustrated by Julie Nicholson

p

One sunny day, a small puppy sat in a grassy garden, watching Snowball and Snowdrop, his brother and sister, play. His coat was white with a few brown patches — and he had one brown paw.

When he was born, his mom said, "He looks like he forgot to put his other socks on!"

And that is how Socks got his name.

"Can I play too?" barked Socks.

"No, you can't!" Snowball yapped back.

"He looks like he's had a mud bath, with those brown splotches," sneered Snowdrop. "Go wash yourself properly, Socks."

"Maybe we should wash him," laughed Snowball. And the two puppies chased Socks toward the birdbath.

Socks ran away as fast as he could
and hid inside the shed — why didn't
they like him? Was it because he
didn't look like them?

A big tear fell from his eye and
trickled down his nose.

Then the two bouncy
puppies appeared.

"Socks, where are you?"
barked Snowdrop.

Socks peeked out
from behind the shed.

"We're going to the woods for a walk,
Socks," called Snowball. "Bye-bye!"

Socks couldn't help it. He ran out onto the
lawn. "Can I come too? Please?" he begged.

"You're much too young to come with us," said Snowdrop. "And you know Mom says you're too young to go out without her."

"I'm not too young," whined Socks. "I've been out lots of times."

"Well, you can't walk with us," said Snowball.
"You must walk behind us."

"Okay," yapped Socks eagerly.

So the two pups scampered through the garden
gate, with Socks following.

Snowball and Snowdrop ran down the lane toward the woods—and Socks trotted behind them!

In a clearing,
there were two paths to
choose from. Snowball's nose
began to twitch. He could smell
something wonderful.

"This way!" he yelped, and the two
older pups rushed off.

"Don't those two ever stop
to look where they're
going?" wondered Socks,
as he lifted his brown
paw and followed.

Around a bend, the puppies
found a huge clump of
beautiful, pink flowers.
Socks pushed his
soft, black nose
into them.

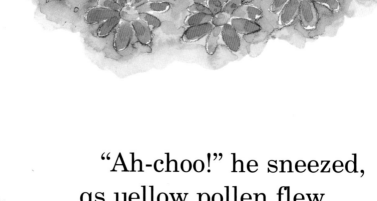

"Ah-choo!" he sneezed,
as yellow pollen flew
into the air.

Snowdrop was
busy chasing a
butterfly.
It fluttered
away down
another
path, and
Snowdrop
followed.

"Come on, Socks!" barked Snowball. "Keep up with us!" And he set off after his sister.

"We'll get lost if we're not careful," thought Socks.

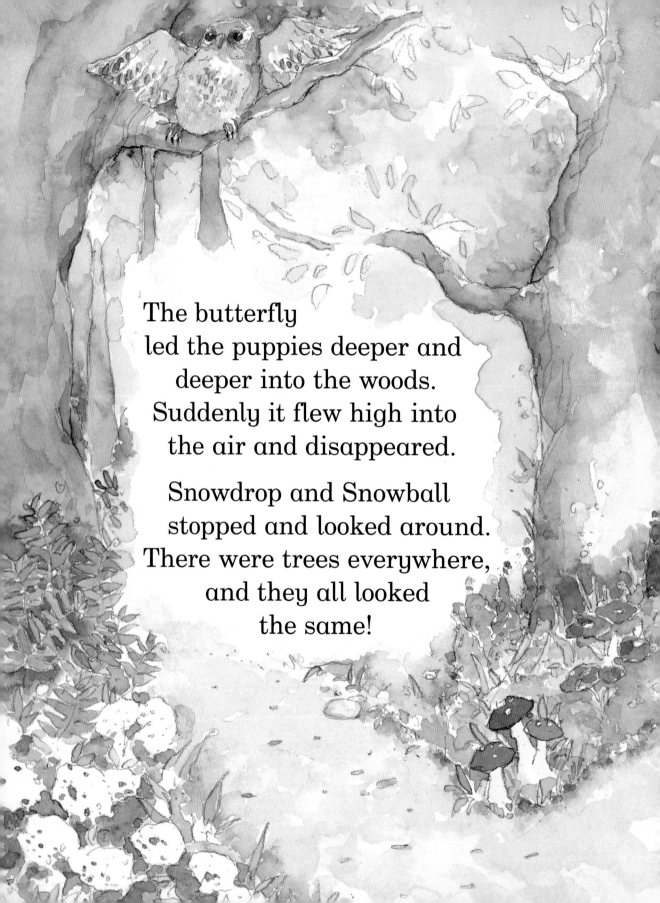

The butterfly
led the puppies deeper and
deeper into the woods.
Suddenly it flew high into
the air and disappeared.

Snowdrop and Snowball
stopped and looked around.
There were trees everywhere,
and they all looked
the same!

"How are we going to
find our way home now?"
wailed Snowball.

"Listen," woofed Snowdrop.
"There's someone through those trees.
Let's see if they know the way home."

"I know the way…"
began Socks.

But Snowball and
Snowdrop weren't
listening. They had
already dashed off along
the path.

"It's easy," thought Socks, and he
set off after the others.

Tap-tap! Tap-tap!

A woodpecker was trying to find some insects in a tree.

"Can you help us find our way home?" asked Snowball and Snowdrop.

But the woodpecker flew off!

"What are we going to do now?"
whined Snowdrop. "I want my mommy!"

"Help!" they howled. "Help!"

"But *I* know the way home!" said Socks.

Snowdrop and Snowball turned to their brother
and stared. "What did you say?" they asked.
"I said I know the way home," Socks said again.
"How?" asked Snowball.

"It's easy," said Socks. "Every time we chose a path, we took the one on the side of my brown paw. To get home, we just turn around and take the path on the side of my white paw. Follow me and I'll show you."

So back through the woods they
went, with Socks in front.
Each time they had to
choose, Socks held up
his brown paw...

... turned his head, and
took the other path.

Back they scampered
through the woods,
past the pink flowers...

... down the lane...

… through the gate, and into the garden,
where their mom was waiting for them.

"Where have you been?"
she woofed angrily.
"I've been so
worried."

"We got lost," said Snowball and Snowdrop.
"It was all our fault."

"Socks was so smart," woofed Snowball.
"We're so lucky to have him as a brother."

"I wish I had a brown paw like him," said Snowdrop. "Do you want to play ball, Socks?"

"Oh, yes!" he woofed, flicking the ball across the lawn to his brother and sister. Sometimes it was good to be different!